A novelization for young readers by B.B. Hiller.
Based on the story by Christopher Reeve
and Lawrence Konner & Mark Rosenthal, and
screenplay by Lawrence Konner & Mark Rosenthal.

SCHOLASTIC INC.
New York Toronto London Auckland Sydney

WARNER BROS. PRESENTS
CHRISTOPHER REEVE · GENE HACKMAN
IN A CANNON GROUP-GOLAN/GLOBUS PRODUCTION OF A SIDNEY J. FURIE FILM SUPERMAN IV
JACKIE COOPER · MARC McCLURE · JON CRYER · SAM WANAMAKER · MARK PILLOW WITH MARIEL HEMINGWAY
AND MARGOT KIDDER AS LOIS LANE VISUAL EFFECTS SUPERVISOR HARRISON ELLENSHAW DIRECTOR OF PHOTOGRAPHY ERNEST DAY, B.S.C. PRODUCTION DESIGNER JOHN GRAYSMARK
ASSOCIATE PRODUCERS MICHAEL KAGAN AND GRAHAM EASTON STORY BY CHRISTOPHER REEVE AND LAWRENCE KONNER & MARK ROSENTHAL
SCREENPLAY BY LAWRENCE KONNER & MARK ROSENTHAL PRODUCED BY MENAHEM GOLAN AND YORAM GLOBUS DIRECTED BY SIDNEY J. FURIE

TM & © DC COMICS INC. 1987

DISTRIBUTED BY WARNER BROS.
A WARNER COMMUNICATIONS COMPANY
© 1987 Cannon Films Inc., Cannon International B.V., and Warner Bros. Inc.

ISBN 0-590-41194-2

12 11 10 9 8 7 6 5 4 3 2 1   7 8 9/8 0 1 2/9
                                                           11

Printed in the U.S.A.

First Scholastic printing, July 1987

For Andrew Neil Hiller

1

Clark Kent could see the cloud of dust moving down the road. It meant somebody was driving up to the Kent farm in Smallville. Clark had only a few minutes until the car arrived. And in those few minutes, he had to do something very important.

Quickly he ran into the barn. He had to hide the capsule which had brought him from Krypton to Earth when he was a baby. His life as Clark Kent was only a disguise. In reality, he was Superman. It was important to keep that a secret; otherwise, he would not be able to live and work with the people of his adopted planet, Earth.

His Kryptonian parents, Jor-El and Lara, had sent him away from Krypton only seconds before that planet exploded forever. He traveled across the universe for years in a special space capsule. When he'd arrived on Earth, he'd been adopted by George and Martha Kent, who had raised him as their own. Now, both his Earth parents were dead and Clark had to sell their farm. Mr. Hornsby, the real estate agent, was driving the car coming up the road.

With super-speed, Clark dug a deep hole in the barn. When he was satisfied it was big enough, he dragged the dusty Kryptonian capsule out of the hayloft and placed it gently in the hole. Just before he began to cover it, he noticed a soft green light glowing in the capsule's control panel.

How could that be? He'd removed everything from the capsule years ago! Nevertheless, it was glowing.

Suddenly, there was a voice. It was his father — Jor-El: "Placed aboard this vessel is an energy module — all that remains of a once powerful civilization. It is my last gift to you. Once removed, the ship will grow cold and silent, and you will be finally alone. The power in the module can be used but once. Use it wisely . . . my son."

Then, there was silence. Clark realized, as he had never before, that he was alone. Krypton was gone. The Kents were gone.

But he didn't have time to think about that. He took the glowing green module from the capsule and tucked it in his pocket. Then, with super-speed, he wound the pile of dirt into a whirlwind which filled the hole and hid his capsule forever.

Mr. Hornsby's car pulled into the driveway. "Hi, Clark," Mr. Hornsby greeted him. "I've got some great news. I've got an offer for the farm and all the land. The buyer made a great offer without even *seeing* the old place."

Clark knew what that meant. Anybody who didn't care what the farm looked like was just going to tear it down — probably for a development like a shopping center. "I'm sorry, Mr. Hornsby. I can't agree to that. Whoever buys this farm has to want to keep it a working farm."

"Gosh, Clark!" Mr. Hornsby began, but he could see it was no use. Clark's mind was made up. Mr. Hornsby shrugged and looked into the barn. "Oh, my, oh my! I remember this," he said, pointing to a dusty old crib whose thick oak headboard had been cracked perfectly in two. "What a joker your old dad was," he chuckled to himself. "I asked George one day what had happened to this thing. 'Oh, Clark must have kicked it,' he said to me."

"Dad always liked a good joke," Clark said laughing, but he was a little uncomfortable with the subject. He wanted to change it. He spotted his old high school baseball glove and bat.

"Say, look at these!" he said. Mr. Hornsby's eyes lit up as he reached for the equipment.

"Batter up, Clark!" He gave Clark the bat, taking the glove and ball for himself. He got into position and pitched to Clark. For a second, Clark was tempted to hit the ball across the fields and into the next county. Instead, he took a giant swing and missed the ball. "Oh, yeah," Mr. Hornsby said, remembering. "You never could hit a curve ball, could you?"

Clark shook his head and changed the subject. "I'll wait until you find a real farmer," he reminded Mr. Hornsby.

The real estate agent nodded and climbed into his car. "Be careful in that big city, Clark. You're a long, long way from where you were born," he said.

"I never forget that, sir," Clark said, knowing Mr. Hornsby couldn't know how far from home he *was*. Mr. Hornsby turned his car around and drove away from the Kent farm.

Clark picked up the bat and ball. He tossed the ball gently in the air and swung the bat at it with all his might.

CRACK! the bat struck the ball.

"Home run!" Clark yelled, happily watching the ball sail endlessly into the sky.

2

Back in Metropolis, Clark was in a hurry again. He had to get to work right away. Lois Lane, star reporter for the *Daily Planet*, where Clark also worked, had called him. She had told him that their boss, Perry White, wanted everybody at a meeting at nine o'clock on the dot. Clark wasn't going to make it.

He was in the subway station, and it was packed. First, he had to wait to buy a token. Then, he had to wait to go through the turnstile. Then, just when it was his turn to go to the platform, a train pulled out of the station. Clark had known he would miss it, but Lois had gotten on it. She'd seen Clark and waved to him as she got on the train.

Superman could fly to work, but Clark had to take the subway. He watched sadly as Lois' train headed for midtown. But something told Clark to watch more carefully. He aimed his X-ray vision down the subway tunnel and searched carefully.

He saw lots of people going to work. He saw hundreds of students going to school. He saw —

Wait a minute! he said to himself. He saw the subway engineer clutching his chest in great pain. He was having a heart attack! If the engineer wasn't running the train, who was? It would surely crash!

Clark dashed along the subway platform so fast that many people only felt a slight breeze as he passed them. As he ran, he changed from his pinstriped suit to his *real* work clothes — the familiar blue and red outfit of *Superman!*

Superman took off along the subway tracks, following the disaster-bound train. In an instant, he'd caught up to the rear car, but he had to get to the front to do his job. He flew between the moving cars and the dingy walls of the tunnel, heading for the engineer's cab. He paused only to wink at an astonished Lois when he passed her.

By the time he reached the front car, the engineer was completely unconscious, and the train was only a few hundred yards from a fatal impact with another subway train. Superman had to stop both trains at once!

He positioned himself on the tracks between the trains and stuck his foot onto the "third rail," the cable which carried millions of volts of electricity to run the subways. Superman drew every watt of the power into himself, draining the entire system and stopping the trains from a catastrophic collision.

Superman carefully guided the trains through the darkened subway into the next station. Confused passengers stepped off the cars. Superman rescued the engineer and told the surprised emergency team, "I'll take this man to the hospital."

Lois stepped out of the train as well. She was just in time to see Superman's cape disappear up the subway stairs, where he carried the engineer. She knew that, once again, Superman had saved her life.

3

A group of prisoners were chained together to prevent escape. They were working in the hot Florida sun, shoveling mud. As they worked, they all sang a sad country-western song.

All except one. He was whistling — could it be? — *Mozart!* It was none other than Lex Luthor, brilliant archcriminal. Lex Luthor had used his genius for crime and the destruction of Superman. Now, he was using it to move slime in a stone quarry.

While the other men worked, Lex stared at the muck. "Life itself began in a murky pool much like this," he said to his fellow prisoners, "and a genius such as myself learns to seize the moment. You are the first to know that I now have a plan to recreate life itself!"

Lex loved to have people admire his superior intelligence. He looked at the rest of the chain gang. He was waiting for applause. He got empty stares. They had no idea what he was talking about. Lex shook his head sadly. "Surrounded by Neanderthals!" he complained.

Just then, a car pulled up near the chain gang. It was a big white Cadillac convertible. The top was down and music blared from the sound system. It could be heard three counties away. A young man, dressed in snakeskin stretch pants and a leopard-print jacket, with a set of earphones around his neck, stepped out.

"Yo, Pops," he said to the two marshals who were guarding the prisoners. "Where on Earth am I, and how do I get to Fort Lauderdale?"

"Son, you're on the wrong side of the state," one of the marshals smirked. He walked over to the car and touched it lovingly. "You got yourself one heck of a car there, son." The other marshal came over to the car, too.

The young man smiled, happy to have them admire his car and sound system. "Go on, get in," he invited them. He didn't have to say it twice. The marshals jumped in happily. They'd never been in such a fancy car in their lives.

"Hot dog!" one marshal said.

"Amen!" agreed the other.

The marshals fiddled with the dials on the sound deck, and ran their hands over the leather upholstery. Nearby, the young man was busy. Very busy.

He pulled a portable mini-tape deck from his pocket and turned it over. It wasn't a tape deck at all. It was a remote controller for the car. He

flipped some switches and rotated a dial. Suddenly, the top went up on the car, the windows rolled up, and the doors snapped locked. The engine roared to life.

"What's going on?" one of the marshals yelled. The young man just smiled sweetly. He could barely hear them. He pushed one more button on the remote, and the Cadillac sailed down the highway. The young man and the chain gang watched it disappear. The prisoners cheered.

The young man turned to Lex Luthor. "Did I do okay, Uncle Lex?" he asked.

"Lenny, I've always thought of you as the Dutch elm disease of our family tree, but this time, nephew, you did fine."

Using wire clippers, Lenny cut the chains which held Lex to the rest of the gang. The two of them began to walk away.

"How about giving us a break, too?" one of the prisoners yelled.

Lex was shocked. "Just because I use my genius in criminal ways, doesn't mean I'm not a firm believer in law and order. You men belong in prison!" He turned on his heel and stalked away. Lenny followed him breathlessly.

"We gonna skip the country, Uncle Lex?"

"No," Lex told him. "We're going to destroy Superman!"

4

Because Superman had saved the engineer of the subway car, Clark Kent was late to work. He tried to sneak into the meeting without anybody noticing it. He didn't make it.

"You're late, Kent!" Perry White, editor in chief of the *Daily Planet*, bellowed.

"It won't happen again, sir," Clark said, but he knew that wasn't true.

"Ha!" Mr. White didn't think it was true, either.

Clark entered the newspaper's large conference room. All of the reporters and photographers were at one end of the room with Mr. White. At the other end were a perfectly dressed silver-haired man and a beautiful young woman who looked as if she'd stepped off the pages of a fashion magazine.

The silver-haired man was shuffling through the current edition of the *Daily Planet*, grumbling as he did so. "Boring . . . tedious . . . dull!"

Clark sidled over to Lois Lane. "Who's that?" he asked.

"None other than Mr. David Warfield," she whispered.

"You mean that tycoon who owns all those sleazy tabloid newspapers?" Clark asked, astonished.

"Correction," Lois told him. "All those sleazy tabloid newspapers *and* the *Daily Planet*." Clark groaned to himself. If Warfield had bought the *Daily Planet*, that meant he'd turn *it* into a sleazy tabloid, too!

Warfield was speaking. It was just what Clark was afraid of. ". . . and, as of today, *this* paper is going to start making money — with the help of my daughter, Lacy Warfield," he said, introducing the beautiful woman next to him.

Lois leaned over to Clark. "She made *her* money the old-fashioned way," she said. "She inherited it."

Lacy stood up to speak to the group. "Once upon a time, the *Daily Planet* was a nice paper. Now, it's just tired. We're going to have a new layout, and I've brought a sample."

She pulled a small-format newspaper out of her briefcase. On the front was a photograph of an attractive woman in a scanty bikini. Clark couldn't stand the idea of the *Daily Planet* becoming a gossip sheet. He decided to speak to Mr. Warfield.

"Sir, that's not really news," he said.

"Maybe not," he agreed, "but it'll sure sell papers!"

14

Mr. White was having a very hard time. His face had gone from pale to pink to red and now was very near purple. "Mr. White, don't do anything rash," Clark said, trying to calm him.

"*Rash?*" he said. "There's the rash!" he said, pointing to Mr. Warfield. Then he turned to storm out of the room.

Lacy spoke firmly to him. "Mr. White, may I point out that Daddy holds your contract, and you must honor it?" Mr. White left the room. Mr. Warfield followed him.

For a few minutes, nobody spoke. Then Clark stepped forward to Lacy. "Miss Warfield," he said. "I'm sure all of us will try to cooperate with you, but a reporter's first duty is to tell the truth to the public. The people of Metropolis depend on the *Daily Planet*, and we can't let them down." Clark shook her hand and left the room.

Lacy watched him leave and then turned to Lois. "Is he for *real?*" she asked in surprise.

"One hundred percent!" Lois assured her.

"I think he's kind of cute," Lacy said.

"Forget it, princess," Lois said. "He's not your type."

Before she had a chance to wonder just whose type Clark *was*, Mr. White bellowed from his office. "Lois! Get in here. The President's about to speak!"

5

Far away from Metropolis, other people were watching the President speak, too. Things weren't going well with the arms talks, and the whole country was worried.

In a small town in the middle of America, a teacher had turned on the television for her class. They heard the President, too. He ended his speech with the worst possible news. ". . . and because the meetings have failed, we must be sure to win the arms race."

Miss Thomas turned off the television set. The students were upset by the speech. They felt helpless.

"Is there anything we can do?" Miss Thomas asked. Nobody answered. "We can write to our congressmen in Washington, can't we?"

One of the boys shrugged. "Fat lot of good that would do," he said. The other kids in the class agreed with him.

But the idea of a letter made one of the boys, Jeremy, think a little more. Jeremy was a thinker. He was also a dreamer. He liked to think about

16

his world the way it *should* be. Miss Thomas and his friends sometimes thought he spent too much time looking out the window and dreaming. But daydreaming was Jeremy's way.

Jeremy sometimes dreamed about a world where nobody had any bombs. It was the kind of world where nobody made fun of anybody just because they were different. It was a world Jeremy would like to live in. Jeremy thought about the President's speech. He agreed with his classmates that writing his congressman wasn't going to do any good. The only thing that *would* do any good would be if somebody came and took away all the bombs and then —

"Jeremy!" Miss Thomas spoke sharply to him. He knew he'd been staring out the window again. Daydreaming again. "I'm sorry to disturb you," she said. "What would *you* do to keep the world from nuclear build-up?"

Before Jeremy could answer, somebody made fun of him. One girl said, "He's so spaced out, he wouldn't even notice!" The other kids laughed.

Suddenly, Jeremy knew the answer to the question. Much to Miss Thomas' surprise, he stood up and spoke. "I'll tell you who I'd write a letter to that *would* do some good."

"Santa Claus?" somebody teased.

"No, Superman," he told the class. Everybody stared at him. "Look," he said. "Superman is the

17

one guy who could pull it off. Nobody would mess with him. He'll collect all the bombs. Zap! They're history!"

"If you're such a good friend of his, why don't you call him up?" one boy said. Pretty soon, everybody was laughing at Jeremy.

But he'd been laughed at one time too many. He would show them. "Look, you all think you're so cool? Well you'll be cool enough when the world gets vaporized! I'm going to write a letter to Superman and send it to the *Daily Planet*."

That didn't stop the smirks and giggles, but the smirks and giggles didn't stop Jeremy.

"Dear Superman," he began to write.

6

Clark Kent was astonished. Lacy Warfield had just told him that she wanted to work with him on a series of articles about "Metropolis After Hours." Together, they would go to all the hot night spots — dinner, dancing, parties, discos.

"But Lacy!" he told her. "I'm usually in bed by 10:30!" It was no use. Her mind was made up, so he had to do it.

"I know *all* the right places," she assured him. "We'll start tonight at the grand opening of the Metro Club. It's a date!"

Clark couldn't say anything. He had to go along with it. She was the boss.

"A date?" Lois said, walking into Lacy's office.

Clark blushed. "It's just research, actually."

Lois winked at him. That made him blush more. Then Lacy cleared her throat and reminded Lois that she had a reason for being there.

"It's Superman Day at the *Daily Planet*," Lois said. "At least it seems that way. We just had a call from the police that somebody — get this — stole the piece of Superman's hair from the Super-

man Exhibit at the Metropolis Museum. It's amazing what trouble people will go to for a souvenir, isn't it?" Clark wondered about that, but Lois just went on talking. "Then, right after that, we got this letter for Superman, care of me."

Lacy's ears perked up at that. "Superman gets mail here?" she asked.

"Oh, probably just a picture request," Clark said casually. "I'll take care of it if you like, Lois."

"You can take care of it, Clark, but it's not really just a picture request. Read it," she said, handing Clark the letter.

It was Jeremy's letter. Clark read out loud. " 'I don't care if everybody thinks I'm a space cadet. Once you've destroyed all the nuclear missiles in the world, they'll see I was right. Superman can make sure we don't blow ourselves up. Quick and easy. Thanks a lot. I know you'll come through. Your friend, Jeremy.' "

Clark was pale, but neither Lois nor Lacy seemed to notice.

Lois just said, "Poor kid. Oh, well, back to work," and left Lacy's office. Lacy, on the other hand, grabbed for her telephone. "I think there's an angle here," she said, thinking out loud. She punched some numbers into her phone. "Daddy loves a campaign. He'll love this one. The whole world will be waiting for Superman's answer. We'll — oh, hello," she spoke into the phone. "Press room?

Hold the afternoon editions. We've got a hot one."
She slammed down the phone. "Daddy will be *so* proud of me!"

Clark heard her, but he wasn't thinking about the afternoon editions or the campaign.

He had a letter to answer.

7

Once again, Jeremy was daydreaming. He gazed out the window, watching the clouds change shapes. He could see all kinds of pictures in them. He could see lambs playing in a field. He could see lollipops stacked up high. He could see cotton candy. He could see — Superman!

Jeremy was so surprised that he jumped up out of his chair.

"Jeremy, do you have a question?" Miss Thomas asked him.

"I thought I saw, uh, Superman!" he said. His classmates started laughing at him. He looked out the window to show them, but there was nothing there. "I guess I was just dreaming, though." He sat down sadly.

Then there was a knock at the classroom door. Everyone looked over there to see Superman, himself, entering *their* classroom. He was carrying Jeremy's letter.

"I'm sorry to interrupt your lesson, Miss Thomas, but I wanted to answer Jeremy in person."

Everybody turned to look at Jeremy. Nobody

was laughing at him now. He'd never felt so good or so proud in his whole life. He couldn't believe he *wasn't* daydreaming.

"Jeremy," Superman said, standing next to his desk. "This is the most important letter I've ever received, but I'm afraid what you're asking is impossible."

"Why?" Jeremy asked.

"Because I made a vow," Superman told him. "I promised never to interfere with the governments of Earth."

It couldn't be true, Jeremy thought. "But what good is a vow if Earth gets blown away? How could my letter be important if you're not going to do what I asked you to do?"

"I'm going to show this letter to all the leaders of the world. They need to know what the people of Earth want them to do."

Superman turned to leave. Miss Thomas spoke. "I'm sure we all want to thank Superman for taking the time to visit us." Then she turned to Superman. "Thank you. We understand."

He nodded to her and reached for the door.

"Well *I* don't understand!" Jeremy said angrily.

"I'm sorry," Superman told him and left.

Jeremy's words of angry disappointment rang in Superman's ears all the way back to Metropolis. This boy, this dreamer, had a knack for showing Superman the things that were really important.

8

Lex Luthor stood near the control panel just outside of his laboratory. It was part of his new hideout on the top floor of the tallest building in town, Metropolis Tower.

He strutted back and forth, boasting to Lenny about how smart he was. "Do you realize what I can create with a single strand of Superman's hair?" he asked.

Lenny gulped. That was a tough question. "A wig that flies?" he suggested.

Lex sighed. "One look at you, Lenny, and I understand why the dinosaurs' pea-sized brains caused their extinction. This piece of Superman's hair which we stole from Metropolis Museum contains a sample of Superman's genetic material — the building blocks of his body. With just the right amount of nuclear power, I can create a being with all of Superman's powers, but with total loyalty to *me*! Observe!" he commanded.

Within Lex's laboratory stood a nuclear chamber. Lenny could see clouds of steam and multi-colored blinking lights. Lex turned knobs, flipped switches, and shifted gears with a skillful hand. He smiled as he worked. "Now, Lenny, give me the dish." Lenny handed his uncle a covered dish with some goo on it. "What we have here is protoplasm made from Superman's genes. We will bombard it with radioactive cosmic rays and duplicate creation itself in a matter of seconds."

The two of them entered the lab. Lex slid the dish into the nuclear chamber and locked it. Then they left the lab, returning to the control panel. Lex turned knobs with a new fury. Through the thick glass window, they watched the nuclear chamber rock and tilt. To Lex's joy — and Lenny's horror — the mass of protoplasm in it grew and changed shape. In a matter of minutes, it was a human form!

The humanoid broke out of the nuclear chamber and stormed right through the walls of the lab into Lex's apartment. It was a gigantic monster, with fearful muscles. It glanced quickly at Lenny, then turned to Lex.

It spoke its first word: "F-f-f-f-aaaaaaather!"

Lex beamed with pride. He handed the creature a thick piece of steel. The creature snapped it in two like a bread stick. Lex picked up a machine gun and fired at the creature. The bullets bounced off like marshmallows. Lex sighed in happiness.

"Very good. Now, the final test. Let's see if he can fly! I command you to rise."

The creature shot up into the air, breaking through the roof of Lex's apartment. A few minutes later, he dropped back down, bringing plaster dust and broken glass with him.

"Okay, okay, so he needs a little coaching," Lex said. "At least he can fly. Now, let's see what little mischief we can do — just to give Metropolis a taste of my creation: Nuclear Man!" Lex thumbed through the *Daily Planet*. "Aha, here it is," he said, pointing to a headline which read: GRAND OPENING OF METRO CLUB TONIGHT!

"Gee, Uncle Lex. I don't think this guy's much of a dancer," Lenny said, eying Nuclear Man.

"Leonard, let's try to keep your I.Q. a family secret. Before he battles Superman, we have to test him — see how he does with mayhem and destruction." He walked over to a table and picked up a photograph of Superman which he held up so Nuclear Man could see it. "I created you for one reason only," he told Nuclear Man. "I want you to destroy this man!"

Nuclear Man glared at the photograph for a minute. Then a wicked grin came over his misshapen face. He spoke for the second time:

"Yes, F-f-f-aaaaaather!"

9

Clark followed Lacy as she sashayed up to the door at the Metro Club. There was a long line of people who wanted to get in. One couple in particular kept begging to get in. They were honeymooners and wanted to be able to tell their friends back home that they'd been to the Grand Opening of the Metro Club. The doorman just ignored them.

Lacy Warfield didn't wait in lines.

"Good evening, Miss Warfield," the doorman said, opening the door for her.

"I'm with her," Clark explained, following her.

It was very dark and very noisy in the Metro Club. Colored lights flashed everywhere, blinking brightly off of mirrors. The disco music came pounding out of speakers which surrounded the dance floor. There were so many people that it was hard to move. Clark just followed Lacy, saying "Excuse me," to everybody he bumped into. He bumped into a lot of people.

"Come on, Clark, let's dance," Lacy said, taking his hand. They went to the dance floor.

Clark and Lacy danced for a few minutes before a man cut in on them. He wanted to dance with Lacy. Clark was relieved to get out of the crowd for a minute. He had a job to do.

Nobody noticed as Clark zoomed out of the front door, to the end of the line. There, he found the honeymooners. He scooped them up in his arms and zoomed back inside with them, passing the doorman so fast, he only felt a faint breeze. Clark put the astonished couple on the dance floor, smiled at them and said, "I think you're supposed to dance." They did. Clark smiled happily, knowing that the couple's friends back home would now hear about the Grand Opening.

Then Clark spotted Lacy, dancing unhappily with a stranger. He came to her rescue and they danced together. Lacy liked dancing with Clark.

"Don't tell me," she said. "You learned to dance at church socials back in Smallville."

Clark blushed. "Actually, I had a crash course from my mother the night before my Senior Prom." Lacy smiled at him. She was used to rich men who were bored with life. There was something very nice about Clark's Smallville view of life. Lacy had never met anyone quite like Clark before.

While they talked about their hometowns, neither one saw the new arrival in the Metro Club: Nuclear Man!

Lex Luthor's creation brushed through the crowd

and stood on the edge of the dance floor. He was confused by the lights and the sound and all the people. But when he saw Lacy Warfield, everything on Earth became much more confusing. He fell in love with Lacy at first sight!

Nuclear Man was so surprised by this sudden feeling that when a woman bumped into him and said "Hey, cutie, let's boogie," he agreed. But she didn't really want to dance. She wanted to be alone with him. She led Nuclear Man out into the alley behind the Metro Club. He was too confused by his love for Lacy to even notice.

As soon as the woman got Nuclear Man into the alley, she realized she'd bitten off more than she could chew. One look at his gigantic misshapen hulk and she was terrified. She screamed. That frightened Nuclear Man out of his wits.

Inside the Metro Club, on the dance floor, Clark heard the woman's cry. This was no time for dancing. This was time for action.

"Uh, excuse me," Clark said to Lacy. She was stunned as he disappeared into the crowd, re-emerging at the alleyway door as Superman!

Superman saw the terrified woman running to safety. He turned his attention to the creature which had scared her. Nuclear Man picked up a huge garbage can and threw it at Superman. It surprised him and knocked him down. Silently, Superman promised himself he wouldn't be ambushed again. He chased Nuclear Man around a corner — only to be jumped by Nuclear Man. Then Superman knew he had a real fight on his hands.

The two of them met in combat in the Metro Club's parking lot. They exchanged punches. But neither of them hurt the other. For a while, it seemed to Superman that they were equally matched. It surprised him to find somebody with all his super-powers, but he didn't have time to wonder how it had happened.

Suddenly, Superman saw that he could take the advantage over his foe. Nuclear Man yanked a lamp post out of the ground and swung it at Superman with all his force, but Superman deflected his blow. He grabbed the end of the lamp post and began to swing it in a full circle. When he came around to where Nuclear Man stood, he whacked him with the lamp post, lifting him off the ground.

"Home run!" Superman yelled, grinning as Nuclear Man sailed almost endlessly into the night. Superman followed Nuclear Man and watched him land in the middle of the cables at Metropolis' electric transformer. Within seconds, Nuclear Man was almost completely destroyed by millions of volts of electricity. Satisfied at his victory, Superman left the transformer.

He never saw Lenny sweeping up the remains of his uncle's creation and putting them into a jar.

10

Jeremy was beginning to wonder if his letter to Superman had been a good idea after all. It started out as a small idea. Now, it was getting to look like a giant problem. The owner of the *Daily Planet*, David Warfield, had brought him to Metropolis to talk to lots of reporters and to tell them how Superman had let him down. It was one thing to tell Superman he'd been disappointed. It was another thing to tell the whole world.

David Warfield held him by the shoulder and led Jeremy to a platform, where he was surrounded by reporters, cameras, and microphones.

"Go ahead, son. Tell the American public what you told me."

Jeremy's knees shook. "I just said . . ." His voice cracked. He almost whispered the rest of the sentence. "I wished Superman had said 'yes.' "

Warfield turned that into the afternoon edition's headline:

SUPERMAN TO KID: DROP DEAD!

In the offices of the *Daily Planet*, Perry White was bellowing at the top of his voice. Lois and Clark had never heard him so angry.

"I'm through taking it lying down!" he yelled, looking at the afternoon edition of the paper. "If anybody wants me, I'll be downtown!" He stood up and stormed out of his office.

Clark was staring at the headline, too. Lois knew he was upset by it. "There's nothing any of us can do," Lois said. Clark new she was right that they couldn't stop David Warfield from irresponsible reporting, but he was beginning to get the feeling that there *was* something he could do about Jeremy.

He dropped the newspaper on the table and left Lois alone in the room. Clark had some thinking to do and he needed to be alone. On his way out, he nearly bumped into the Warfields. They were escorting Jeremy through the office.

Clark wasn't sure he wanted to see Jeremy. If he'd learned one thing about the boy, it was that Jeremy couldn't be fooled. While Clark hastened down the hall, Jeremy came over and stopped him.

"Excuse me," he said. "Do I know you?"

Clark had to think for a second. It seemed to him that Jeremy knew him very well, indeed. But, of course, the person who Jeremy knew was Superman. "I'm Clark Kent, one of the staff reporters," Clark said.

Jeremy leaned over to Clark. Something about the man's face told him he could trust him. "Do you know Superman?" he whispered. Clark nodded. "Would you tell him I'm sorry? I didn't mean to cause him trouble. Tell him I just want him to do what's right. Please, can you tell him that?"

Clark put a comforting hand on Jeremy's shoulder. "Don't worry," he said. "I'm sure Superman cares a lot more about what's in one boy's heart than in all the newspapers in the world."

"Thanks," Jeremy said, relieved.

Clark was relieved, too. Because now he knew what he had to do.

While Jeremy and the Warfields left for another press conference, Clark removed his glasses and ducked into the men's room. A few seconds later, Superman flew out the men's room window, headed due north.

Superman had some thinking to do and he needed to be alone. Completely alone.

Superman landed on the frozen ground near the North Pole. In front of him was a gigantic moun-

tain of ice and snow. He put his hand on his hips and stamped firmly on the ground. Suddenly, there was an avalanche. All of the ice and snow fell away from the mountain, revealing Superman's retreat — The Fortress of Solitude.

He went into his ice castle, hoping to learn from the wisdom of Krypton, which was stored there. He picked up a crystal and fed it into a "reader." Suddenly, he saw images of the destruction of his home planet. He knew, from the crystals, that his father and mother had known Krypton was going to be destroyed. Yet, they'd stayed there and died with the planet. It was a matter of honor.

"If I don't do something about the weapons on Earth, I'm afraid it will meet an end as terrible as Krypton's!" he said.

A voice came from the crystal. "It is as dangerous for Earth to rely on any one man — even you — as it is for Earth to continue making bombs. You must *not* interfere. It is forbidden."

The last word echoed off the ice walls.

Superman thought about the wisdom of Krypton. Then he thought about the wisdom that a young boy named Jeremy had showed him. He made up his mind.

"You have taught me well. But sometimes, there is more to learn from children than the wisest of men. Farewell."

He was ready to return to Metropolis.

11

Superman circled Metropolis until he found Jeremy. The boy was with Jimmy Olsen, the *Daily Planet*'s young photographer. Jimmy was showing him around the city.

Jeremy was about to bite into a big hot dog when — WHOOSH! — Superman landed next to him.

"Would you like to take a walk with me?" Superman asked.

"You bet!" Jeremy replied.

Together, they walked across town to the only place where Superman could speak to all the people of Earth at once: the United Nations. Superman's message wasn't just for one or two countries. It was for everybody.

By the time they arrived at the world headquarters of the United Nations, they had a big crowd following them, including reporters. The whole world was curious.

When they reached the door of the General Assembly, two guards stopped them, briefly.

"I don't think he has a pass," one said.

"I don't think he *needs* a pass," the other replied. The guards opened the doors for Superman and Jeremy.

Superman showed Jeremy how to get to the Visitors' Gallery and then he went to the front of the room. As Superman walked past the delegates, he was reminded, once again, how many *different* people lived on this planet — his home. He saw people of all colors, all sizes, all nations, all religions. There were men and women. They spoke hundreds of languages. But they all had one thing in common. They wanted peace. Yet, they didn't seem to be able to achieve it.

Superman stood up at the microphone and spoke to all of Earth's governments.

"For many years, I've lived among you as a visitor. But now, Earth is my home, too. We cannot live in fear of a war that would destroy our home. I have come to a decision."

Excited, the delegates sat forward in their seats. Jeremy could hardly believe his ears.

Superman went on. "I am going to do what your governments have been unable to do. I will take away and destroy all the nuclear weapons on this planet, Earth."

From the balcony, the delegates heard Jeremy yell, *"All right!"*

Then everybody joined in. The whole world was cheering.

12

Superman dived into the Pacific Ocean. He had tracked a submarine which carried nuclear bombs. He found the boat and took the bombs from it. He flew them high into the sky, beyond the reach of Earth's gravity. There, he had constructed a giant net to hold all the bombs he'd collected until he was ready to destroy them.

He returned to Earth for another load. This time, he went to Russian Siberia. There, he found a missile on a launcher. He plucked it from the launch pad and rode it high into the sky. Then, he put it in the net with the other bombs.

Superman closed the net tightly and took the entire load of bombs — hundreds of them — and flew directly toward the sun. He knew that the sun, itself, was merely a gigantic nuclear furnace. The explosion of a few hundred nuclear bombs from Earth would make no difference to the sun. Superman threw the netful of bombs directly into the sun. They were destroyed immediately and forever. Superman returned to Earth for another load.

While Superman was destroying bombs, Lex Luthor was figuring out how to destroy Superman. He thought he had a pretty good idea, but he needed a little bit of help from some friends.

"Allow me to introduce you to one another," Lex said to the three men who sat in his apartment. "First, we have Harry Howler, nuclear strategist for America's top think tank and a great warmonger in his own right." Lex pointed to a nervous man, dressed in a wrinkled suit which barely covered his oversized body.

"Next we have Jean-Pierre DuBois," Lex said, pointing to a distinguished-looking man. "Monsieur DuBois sells nuclear bombs to anybody who has the money for them." DuBois glared at Lex. He didn't trust him.

"And finally," Lex said, pointing to a portly man in a Russian general's uniform. "General Romoff, known to some as the Mad Russian because he keeps trying to get his country into a war."

The three men glared at each other suspiciously. Lex went on talking. "I know you're all really thrilled that Superman is ending the nuclear arms race, right?" Of course, that wasn't true at all. Superman was going to put them all out of business.

The three men slumped in their chairs. "Get to the point!" Harry Howler grunted.

"The point is that I, Lex Luthor, the greatest

criminal mind of the modern era, have discovered a way to destroy Superman! Right here, in this dish, is a sort of 'genetic stew.' " He held up the dish in which he had stored the remains of Nuclear Man. But even those remains had Superman's genes. If Lex could get enough nuclear power to make those genes grow into a living creature, it would be able to destroy Superman. "Boys," he said to the three men, "if you help me place this dish on one of your missiles and then Superman throws it into the sun, *that* will be all the nuclear power I need. Superman will get the biggest surprise of his life: Nuclear Man. Then, with the end of Superman, you boys will be back in business — "

"What's in it for *you*?" DuBois asked.

Lex smiled slyly. "Oh, I'll just take a tiny commission on your sales. Something appropriate, you know. Perhaps a few million dollars?"

They didn't like it, but they had no choice.

13

When Superman carried the next missile into space, he had no idea what he was *really* doing.

Lex Luthor had given Harry Howler the dish with Nuclear Man's genes on it. Harry had tricked a general into hiding the dish in the next bomb that Superman was scheduled to destroy.

Superman carried that bomb to his giant net of bombs in space and when the net was full, he hurled it into the sun. Superman returned to Earth right away. He never even noticed that that load caused a much bigger explosion than the others.

Behind Superman's back, the flames from the explosion on the sun licked millions of miles into space. One of the flames jumped away from the others and began sailing toward Earth. As it came, it began to change shape. It seemed to grow arms and legs, a head and a body. What a body! Even the creature paused to admire his own beautiful muscular human shape as he flew toward Earth. But he didn't pause for long. He had inherited the first Nuclear Man's memory. He knew everything that his predecessor had known. Right then, he knew that he had to find Lex Luthor — the man known to his genes as F-f-f-aaaaaather!

Down in Metropolis, Lex waited impatiently, but he didn't have to wait long.

Suddenly, there was a WHOOSH! and the new, improved Nuclear Man landed on the deck of Lex's skytop apartment. Nuclear Man seemed to have come on a beam of light and stood in the window, surrounded by sunlight. Lex looked at him and he was aghast.

"He's beautiful. Perfect. And I'm incredible!" Lex said as he circled his creation. He was frequently in awe of his own accomplishments. "First things first," he told Nuclear Man. "I want to give you a few tests — check out your reflexes."

Lex took a metal ruler and prodded Nuclear Man with it. Nuclear Man didn't like that. He hissed and grew red with anger. The metal ruler *melted*.

"Oh, my," Lex said. "The nuclear power has made *him* a furnace. I like it! I am sooooo smart! I am — " he searched for a word.

Nuclear Man supplied it: "Nothing. You are nothing!" he told Lex. "*I* am Father now." This wasn't quite what Lex had in mind.

"You're just an experiment — a *freako!*" Lenny said to Nuclear Man.

Suddenly, Lenny found himself lifted into the

air and flying in circles in Lex's apartment. Somehow, Nuclear Man was controlling him. Lenny was totally helpless. Nuclear Man turned to Lex. "Am I just an experiment? A freako?" he asked.

Lex shrugged. "I made you, and I can destroy you," Lex told him, though he wasn't at all sure it was true.

"Destroy?" Nuclear Man said, repeating the word. There was something he remembered, but not clearly. He said it again. "Destroy." He was quiet for a second, then his eyes lit up — a bright red. "Destroy Superman now!"

"You remembered, you sweet thing," Lex said proudly. "Not quite yet, though. Come on inside and we'll discuss it." He invited Nuclear Man into his apartment.

Lenny was still flying around in circles helplessly. "I was just goofing around!" he yelled at Nuclear Man, trying to apologize. Nuclear Man didn't seem interested. "If anybody's a freako around here," Lenny called, "it's me!" Nuclear Man released him. Lenny crashed to the floor. Lex barely noticed.

Lex walked into the hallway of his apartment. Nuclear Man followed — up to a point. Suddenly, he wasn't moving. He was frozen like a statue. Lex turned and stared at him. He touched the creature's skin. "He's cold!" he said in surprise.

His mind raced, searching for an explanation.

"Of course!" he said. "That's his one vulnerability! The one way he can be stopped!"

"What?" Lenny asked.

Lex glared at Lenny. "Leonard, my loud-mouthed nephew," he said. "Nuclear Man gets his power from sunlight. In darkness, he's like you. He's useless!"

14

Once again, Clark Kent was someplace he didn't want to be, just because Lacy Warfield wanted him to be there. He was in an exercise class at a fancy health club. While everyone else in the class was wearing sleek clothes, Clark was wearing baggy sweat pants and a sweat shirt. While everybody else jumped and stretched in time to the music, Clark was trying to catch up. The class turned right. Clark turned left. His glasses slipped down on his nose. He sighed.

"Don't give up!" Lacy said. "This health club is a perfect subject for your new series of stories on young Metropolis!"

Clark tried again. He was having a hard time. It wasn't easy pretending to be a klutz!

A few minutes later, they were in the room with the exercise machines. These were supposed to build strong bodies. Lacy showed Clark how to do it. "Now you try, Clark. We'll start you off with 60 pounds."

Clark sat on the bench and strained to lift the

weights. He couldn't do it. In fact, it sort of backfired and the next thing Lacy knew, Clark had been thrown to the floor.

"Need some help?" somebody asked. Clark looked to see who it was. His name was Paul. He was a club member who had been watching Clark struggle with the classes and the equipment. He thought it was pretty funny that Clark was such a klutz. "I guess your friend doesn't know his own strength," he said to Lacy smirking. He gave Clark a hand to help him stand up.

"Want to try this weight, Clark?" he asked, lifting a gigantic weight bar with four heavy weights attached. He offered it to Clark.

"I don't think so," Clark told him. But Paul gave it to him anyway. Clark grasped the bar, but the weight pulled him and the barbell right to the floor of the health club with a noisy THUNK! Everybody in the room laughed at him.

"No pain, no gain," Paul said smugly. He sauntered off.

Clark looked after him helplessly. "He's a jerk," Lacy said, trying to make Clark feel better. It didn't seem to help much. She helped Clark stand up and then decided to change the subject. "Say, Clark, Lois is doing an interview with Superman about his peace mission. It's going to be at my apartment. I want you to be there, too."

"Me?" Clark said, aghast.

"Yes. Come tonight at five o'clock." She left him then to shower and get dressed.

Clark was trapped, and he knew it. After all, Lacy was the boss. But how could Superman and Clark be in the same place at the same time? He was so worried about the problem that he barely noticed when Paul came back for some more jokes at Clark's expense.

"Say, Clark," Paul said smirking again. "Could you hand me those weights over there? They're very light." He pointed to a three hundred pound barbell.

Without thinking, Clark picked it up easily and tossed it to Paul. The heavy weight knocked Paul completely off his feet and pinned him on the floor.

When Clark realized what he'd done, he looked at Paul and shrugged.

"No pain, no gain," he said.

15

Lacy and Lois were excited about their dinner party for Clark and Superman.

The doorbell rang. "Oh, Clark's here," Lacy said. "Or maybe it's Superman."

"Superman likes to make a different kind of entrance," Lois reminded her.

Lacy opened the door. It was Clark. "I need change for the taxi cab," he said. "Can you break a twenty dollar bill?" Lacy gave him the money and he left. "I'll be back in a flash," he promised them.

Just a few seconds later, there was a slight rush of wind on the terrace. "What's that?" Lacy asked.

"Our other dinner guest," Lois told her. She went to greet Superman.

She brought Superman into Lacy's living room and they both sat down on the sofa so Lois could start her interview.

But Lacy was worried about Clark. Where *was* he? "I'd better go downstairs and fetch Clark. He's probably helping the cab driver change a flat tire or doing some other good deed!" Superman had thought he'd have a few minutes rest, but now he had to figure out a way to be Clark again. What would Lacy think if she got down to the lobby and Clark had disappeared? He had to think fast.

He sniffed the air. "Something smells good," he said.

Lois blushed a bit. "Just a little duck and scallops Lacy and I cooked — in case we get hungry later." She was flattered that Superman had noticed, but then Superman noticed *everything*. "Now, to the interview," she said, taking out the list of questions David Warfield had given her to ask Superman. "Have you had any trouble getting the missiles?"

"Well, Lois, there is always the chance that a few warped individuals would take advantage of the world's goodwill," he began. As he continued speaking, however, his mind, and some of his powers, turned to something else: the oven. He used his heat vision to raise the temperature from 350 degrees to 650 degrees. In a matter of seconds, the duck was sizzling.

"Oh, my!" Lois said, sniffing. "Dinner! Don't budge. I'll be right back." She ran out of the room. Superman budged.

Quick as a wink, he flew downstairs, changing into Clark's suit on the way. He met Lacy in the lobby.

"There you are, Clark," she said. "Come on up-stairs. Superman's already there." She took him by the arm and led him back to the elevator. When the elevator door opened Lacy stepped right into it. Clark, on the other hand, had gotten caught up with somebody moving luggage off the elevator. Before he could extract himself from the tangle, the elevator door closed and Lacy was on her way back to the penthouse without him.

Lois found Superman on the balcony, admiring the view. When Lois returned to the living room, Lacy was letting herself back in. She was alone.

"Where's Clark?" Lois asked.

Lacy seemed a little bit frustrated. "Well, he was getting on the elevator, and then this man with luggage . . . and oh, it's a long story," Lacy said.

Lois nodded. "It always is with Clark."

The doorbell rang. It was Clark. "Hi, is dinner ready?" he asked. "I'm starved!"

Lois decided she could finish her interview later. After all, dinner was ready. "Superman!" she called out onto the balcony. There was no answer. "I'll get him," she said, heading for the balcony. But then there was a loud crash. Clark had knocked into a tray of wine glasses. It was a disaster. Lois and Lacy began the clean-up. Clark excused himself, explaining he'd spilled wine on his suit.

A few seconds later, Superman was standing

on the balcony again, his worst suspicions realized. He'd thought there was some funny business going on with an advertising billboard he could see from Lacy's balcony. Now, he knew he was right. The billboard no longer showed an ad for cigarettes. It showed none other than Lex Luthor.

"Hi, there, Blue Boy," Lex greeted him from the screen. "Don't worry. You're the only one who can hear me. It's my own television network."

Superman dreaded Lex's message. He stared at the screen in front of him.

"Look to your right," Lex said, pointing to Metropolis Tower. "I'm about to blow twenty stories off — give or take a floor or two."

As suddenly as it had appeared, the image disappeared. There was the cigarette ad once again.

Superman knew that whatever Lex was up to, he couldn't ignore it. He couldn't risk the lives of the innocent citizens of Metropolis.

"I'm terribly sorry, Lois," he said to her. She had stepped onto the balcony to tell him dinner was ready. "An emergency has arisen. Please apologize to your guests. Good night!"

He flew from the balcony toward Metropolis Tower.

"Wait! Tell me! I'll cover it for the paper!" Lois called after him.

But he was gone.

16

Superman circled Metropolis Tower, examining every inch of it with his X-ray vision. There was no sign of a bomb, but there *was* a sign of Lex Luthor. He stood on his terrace and waved to Superman.

"Guess who? It's your old friend, Lex."

"Luthor," Superman said, landing on the terrace, too. "I suspect if you had actually planted a bomb, you'd be far away from here by now."

"Silly me," Lex said, brushing his cheek with his hand. "How do I ever think I can fool the super-guy. You're right. No bomb. I just invited you here because I want to be the first one to introduce you to the new kid on the block."

Suddenly, there was a blinding flash of light. It came down from the sky. On Lex's terrace, the light assembled itself into Nuclear Man. He was glowing so fiercely that he melted the steel safety railing on the terrace.

Superman had never seen anything quite like Nuclear Man. He examined him carefully with his X-ray vision.

"Look closely at his cells," Lex said. "See anything familiar?" Then, Superman understood. "You've broken all the laws of man, Luthor. And now you've broken the laws of nature! I assume you must have hidden a device in one of the missiles I destroyed in the sun."

Lex clapped his hands. "You know, Mr. Muscle," he said, "I'll really miss these chats we've had. Now that Einstein is dead, you're the only one who can keep up with me."

Just then, Lenny stepped out onto the terrace. He leered at Superman. "Boy are you going to get it!" he said.

Nuclear Man thought that was his cue. "Destroy Superman!" he roared.

"Not quite yet!" Lex curbed him. He turned to Superman. "He's anxious to start. Can you blame him?"

"Your time in prison has twisted your mind further, Luthor," Superman said.

"No, listen," Lex explained. "I escaped with only one thing on my mind: the end of Superman. So I created a monster who didn't work nearly as well as I might have liked."

Superman recalled his battle with the first Nuclear Man. "Which explains why you sent *his* genes to the sun."

"Precisely," Lex said. "Then I made a deal with some minor league bad boys. Arms dealers, renegade generals. You know the type. With you gone, we'll make a fortune re-arming the world."

Superman was aghast. "You'd risk worldwide nuclear war for your own personal financial gains?" he asked.

Lex shook his head. "Nobody wants war. I just want to keep the threat alive. That way, people buy lots of bombs — particularly if somebody has just thrown a whole lot of them away. Get it?"

"A mind is a terrible thing to waste, Lex Luthor. And you've wasted yours on this foul monstrosity. I'm taking you in!" Superman reached for Lex.

Suddenly, Nuclear Man stretched to become twice his normal size. He glowed so hot that his body smoked. Then, he returned to his normal size.

"Nifty, huh?" Lex asked. Superman didn't answer. "Well, good night, sweet prince." He turned to Nuclear Man. "Now destroy Superman."

Nuclear Man's eyes glowed with joy. "First, I have fun," he declared, rising into the sky and taking off.

17

Superman took off after Nuclear Man. He had the feeling that Nuclear Man's idea of "fun" could mean disaster for the world. In a few seconds, he learned he was right.

Nuclear Man's first stop was in the middle of America. He stopped at a small town, a few houses and a church, surrounded by farms. It reminded Superman of Smallville and of Jeremy's hometown. But this town was in trouble. Nuclear Man began flying in a circle so quickly and so fiercely that he created a deadly tornado. And the tornado was heading directly for a farmhouse.

Superman saw a family — mother, father, and two children — escape from the farmhouse and head for the safety of their storm cellar. Just before the cellar door shut, though, the mother cried out, "Jenny's inside!" and pointed to the house. The tornado picked up the entire house and began to spin it fiercely. In seconds, it was surrounded by a cloud of dust. Superman dived into the whirlwind, took hold of the farmhouse, and began circling in the opposite direction. As Nuclear Man had *started* the storm by spinning in one direction,

Superman finished it by spinning the other way.

He set the house back down on its foundation and ran inside to rescue Jenny. The two-year-old girl was frightened, but safe. Gently, he carried her to her mother's arms. He would have liked to stay, but Nuclear Man was on his way, and Superman had to catch him. He saluted the farmer and his family and took off.

Nuclear Man's next stop was the Great Wall of China. It had taken millions of workers hundreds of years to build. Nuclear Man was destroying it in a matter of seconds. Tourists were tumbling off it. As soon as Superman arrived, Nuclear Man began hurling hundreds of stones and bricks at him. Superman knocked them aside. Then, he turned to help the tourists. Nuclear Man fled while Superman put the Wall back together again. In a few minutes, the tourists waved their thanks to Superman, and he took off after Nuclear Man again.

When Nuclear Man made a volcano erupt, Superman took the top off of another mountain and dropped it on the lava, corking it shut for good.

When Nuclear Man threatened Russian leaders with a missile carrier, Superman turned it away from them.

Nuclear Man's idea of fun was Superman's idea of Big Trouble. But the biggest trouble was yet to come.

Nuclear Man's next and final stop was Metropolis. He flew to the Statue of Liberty and tugged it off its pedestal. Before Superman could stop him, Nuclear Man released the gigantic Statue over Metropolis. It was going to fall on top of hundreds of people. Superman dived and caught it just seconds before it hit the crowd.

Superman carried the Statue with both hands in order to return it to its place in the city's harbor undamaged. As he flew, however, Nuclear Man appeared on the Statue's torch. If Superman let go of the Statue with one hand to fend off Nuclear Man, he would risk ruining the Statue.

Nuclear Man attacked Superman's hand which gripped the Statue. Nuclear Man ripped Superman's skin with his burning claws. Superman was instantly weakened because the wound made him vulnerable to Nuclear Man's deadly atomic radiation. He had just enough strength to put the Statue back on its pedestal. Then, he collapsed.

Nuclear Man attacked for a final time. He kicked Superman with all his terrible power and sent him sailing into the sky out of sight.

"Bulls-eye!" he yelled, watching Superman disappear into space.

And then Superman's familiar red and blue costume floated back out of the sky empty. It came to rest on the torch of the Statue of Liberty.

18

Lois stared at the newspaper in front of her. The front page of the *Daily Planet* showed a picture of Superman's cape draped on the Statue of Liberty, and the headline read:

IS SUPERMAN DEAD?

Clark hadn't come to work that morning. Mr. White was in some kind of top secret conference. And the new owners of the paper were having a wonderful time, making money off of Superman's troubles. In short, nothing was going right, and Lois wasn't going to take it any more.

She stormed into Lacy's office. Mr. Warfield was there, too.

"This time, you've both gone too far! I *quit!*" Lois announced. She waited for a reaction, but there was none. Then she saw Superman's cape and costume lying on Lacy's desk. "And you sure don't have any right to *this*," she said, picking up the costume. She walked out. For good.

As Lois waited for the elevators, a group of business men stepped off into the corridor. They didn't know where they were going.

"Excuse me," one said to Lois. "Can you tell me where I can find Mr. White?"

Lois looked at the men. Before she had a chance to answer, Perry White rushed down the hallway toward them. "Gentlemen, gentlemen, this way," he said. Lois only had a second to notice that Perry was dressed just like those men. They all — even Perry — looked just like bankers. But Lois was too upset right then to wonder what was going on.

At that moment, Lex Luthor and Harry Howler were meeting with senators and generals in Washington. It was time for Lex's favorite part of his scheme. It was time to make *money*.

Lex started to speak. "Mr. Howler and I are here today because we think you should know that Superman has tricked you!" He waited a minute for that to sink in. They were shocked. "I'm sure I don't have to tell smart people like you that 'world peace' is merely a Communist plot. I mean, how do you *know* that Superman actually destroyed everybody else's missiles? And just exactly where *is* Superman so you can ask him yourself? Don't know, do you? Well, check with your spies in Moscow today!" The men at the table gasped. Could it be true that Superman was plotting *against* the American way?

"Since I'm sure you don't want to risk the safety of this country, Mr. Howler and I would like to be able to provide you with a few strategic weapons — at a very affordable price!"

One of the generals spoke to the other men at the table. "If what he says is true, we'll have to buy some bombs right away!"

Lex Luthor smiled happily. It was music to his ears.

The very next day, Lex stood next to General Romoff in a conference room in Moscow. "Comrades," Lex said. "I'm sure we all know 'world peace' is a capitalist plot . . ."

Lex was succeeding totally in making everybody in the world so afraid of everybody else that they were sure the answer lay in more nuclear bombs. And that was just what Lex was selling.

Two days later, Lex was meeting again with his three favorite warmongers: Howler, Romoff, and DuBois. Everybody was happy as could be since there was a gigantic pile of cash in the middle of the table, and they were at Lex's apartment to split it up.

Lex stood up to speak. Nuclear Man stood next

to him. Howler, Romoff, and DuBois were getting a bad feeling about what Lex was going to say.

"Gentlemen," Lex said. "I've decided to assume full control of all your operations. As my first official act, you're fired." The men gasped in surprise. "And, according to my calculations, your share of the money is — " Lex counted on his fingers, whispering out loud to himself as he did the arithmetic. "Put down the seven, carry the five, plus four is nine and eight is seventeen, put down the seven. Move the decimal two places and it's — " He looked back up at his former partners. "In round numbers it's *zero*. Nothing. Nada. Zippola!"

"You're mad!" Romoff cried.

Coolly, Lex pulled a cigar from his pocket and snapped his fingers. Nuclear Man touched the end of the cigar with his arm and the cigar burst into flame.

Howler, Romoff, and DuBois had seen enough. Dealing with Lex Luthor was one thing, but dealing with Nuclear Man was *another*. They all ran out of Lex's apartment as fast as they could go.

19

Lois was really worried about Clark. She hadn't seen or heard from him in days, and he didn't answer his phone. She was afraid he'd had some kind of awful accident, so she went to his apartment. There was no answer when she knocked at the door or rang the bell. There was only one other thing to do. She picked the lock.

When the door finally opened, Lois was astonished to see Clark. He looked awful! His skin was terribly pale and his eyes were bloodshot. He was holding on to the back of a chair to stand up.

"I knew it!" Lois said. "You're ill!" She walked over to him and helped him back to his couch.

"It's just a bad flu, really," he said. But, looking at him, Lois knew it was more than that.

"Well, I'm sure you know what you're doing. But I had to see you because Superman is in trouble."

"Has something happened to him?" Clark asked, wishing with all his heart that he could tell Lois what was going on.

"Everyone is saying he's dead, but I think he just needs help, Clark."

Once again, Clark was touched by Lois' affection for Superman. She always seemed to understand.

"You know him so well, Lois," he said. "I'm sure he'll manage, though."

"I wish there was a way for me to tell him that I care about him, and I know he's tried his best to help Earth — "

"I know he'd thank you, Lois," Clark said. "But if you'd excuse me, I need to rest by myself now. Please."

Lois didn't want to leave. She thought Clark needed her help, but if he didn't want it, there wasn't much she could do. She was too upset about Superman to argue, anyway.

She stood up to leave. "Feel better soon, Clark," she said. "And, if you should see Superman or hear from him, he might need this." She gave Clark a package and left him alone.

Clark's hands were shaking as he opened the package Lois had given him. It was Superman's costume.

Clark stumbled into his bathroom and looked at the face he saw in the mirror. In all his years on Earth, he had never known pain and weakness such as he felt now. He had never been afraid he might die. He was afraid of all these things now.

Then, while he watched, he suddenly saw himself getting older! His skin wrinkled; his hair turned gray.

Clark looked at the wound which Nuclear Man had made. It was a deep cut on his hand, through skin which he had once thought invulnerable. It wasn't healing; it was only getting worse.

Then Clark remembered his father's last words. They were the words he had heard when he'd buried the capsule which had brought him from Krypton. "Placed aboard this vessel is an energy module. Its power can be used only once. Use it wisely."

This was the time, Clark knew. For if he didn't use it, he would surely die.

Clark went to his closet where he had hidden the module after he'd returned from Smallville. He held it tightly in his hand and switched it on.

Instantly, he could feel its power surging through his weak body.

Would it be enough?

20

The first rays of the morning sun awoke Nuclear Man. And the first thing he saw when his eyes opened was the *Daily Planet*. On the front page, there was a picture of Lacy Warfield. The article explained that she was the new publisher of the paper.

Lacy Warfield. Nuclear Man gaped at the picture. He'd seen the woman before, but his memory wasn't clear. He stared some more. Then it came to him. It wasn't *his* memory. It was the memory of the first Nuclear Man. He had fallen in love with Lacy at first sight when he'd seen her at the Metro Club. The new Nuclear Man felt the same. Right away, he knew that Lacy was the only woman for him.

"Good morning." Lex interrupted Nuclear Man's thoughts when he and Lenny entered the room. "We've got a heavy schedule this morning. We're going into the insurance business. I'm going to insure the world against *you!*"

But Nuclear Man wasn't listening. He had only one thing on his mind, and that was Lacy Warfield. Now that he knew where to find her, he wasn't going to waste a minute. "Wait for my return," he commanded. "I will bring back the girl." With that, he flew off Lex's terrace.

"Gee, Uncle Lex," Lenny said. "I thought you could control that nuclear guy! You really blew it, huh?"

"Shut up, Leonard," Lex said.

Nuclear Man found Lacy at the office of the *Daily Planet*. He crashed through the wall where Lacy and her father were having a conference. When David Warfield tried to protect Lacy, Nuclear Man threw him against a wall.

"Daddy!" Lacy cried, but it was no good. Nuclear Man scooped her up into his arms, and before she knew it, she was in Lex's apartment, totally surprised and totally captive. Lex and Lenny were Nuclear Man's captives, too.

Lex tried to get back into Nuclear Man's good graces. As usual, he was doing it by trying to take the upper hand.

"You know, I'm about out of patience with you. Just say you're sorry, and we'll be friends. Look, we've got the whole world where we want them, sitting on their bomb buttons. Right now, any little blip on the radar would set off a war. It's the perfect time to make a bundle of money!"

Nuclear Man didn't care about money. He only cared about two things: Lacy Warfield and having

fun. Lex had given him an idea of how to have a lot of "fun."

"I'll be back for you," he said to Lacy. Then, his body began to change shape. It became the unmistakable shape of a bomb. A nuclear bomb! Nuclear Man shot into the air.

As soon as Nuclear Man reached flying altitude, he was spotted by military radar.

"Do we have identification?" the Chief of Staff asked the radar technician in Washington.

"It's not ours, sir," he answered, "and they said it's not *theirs*!"

"Can we risk launching?" the Chief asked.

"Can we risk *not* launching?" the general asked in response.

On the other side of the world, three Russian generals clustered around a radar screen.

"What if it's not theirs?" the first one asked.

"What if it *is*?" the second one asked.

The third shook his head sadly. "We haven't given ourselves any other choice," he said. "Prepare to counterattack." The others knew he was right.

Meanwhile, back in Lex's apartment, he and Lenny were getting ready to hide from the nuclear war they were sure Nuclear Man would start.

"Don't worry, honey," Lex said to Lacy. "I'm sure he'll make a swell husband. In the meantime, if you need us, we'll be five hundred feet underground, waiting for the nuclear winter to turn into nuclear spring." He and Lenny carried their suitcases over to the elevator.

But when the elevator door opened, Superman stepped off!

"Superman! But you're dead!" Lex gasped.

"Still having delusions, Lex Luthor?" Superman asked. Then he brushed past Lex to go to Lacy's aid.

"Superman, the monster is going to start a war!" Lacy cried. Then she told him what had happened. Superman knew he didn't have a second to spare, and he could only think of one way to save the world, but he needed Lacy's help.

"I have no right to ask you this," Superman said to Lacy. "It could be dangerous."

"Ask me," Lacy said. "I'll do anything to help."

Superman picked her up and leaped off of Lex's terrace.

In Washington, a general was counting down to launch a counterattack. "Nine . . . Eight . . . Seven . . ."

In Moscow, they were counting down as well. "Six . . . Five . . . Four . . ."

Superman had four seconds to save Earth!

21

uperman held Lacy tightly as they flew over
the ocean to meet up with Nuclear Man. As
soon as Nuclear Man spotted them, Superman
asked Lacy, "Ready?"

"Ready," she told him. "Let's see what I'm made
of."

Superman let go of her. She began falling toward the freezing cold water. Nuclear Man couldn't
stand to see Lacy get hurt. Instantly, he changed
from his bomb shape back to a humanoid.

The change was spotted on radar screens around
the world. "Stop the countdown! It's gone!" the
technician yelled in Washington.

"All systems cease action!" the Russian general
hollered.

Everybody sighed with relief.

Except Superman. He had to rescue Lacy before Nuclear Man got to her. He dived sharply,
catching her only seconds before Nuclear Man
would have had her. Then, before Nuclear Man
could catch him, Superman changed his course.

He took Lacy to Metropolis. Nuclear Man followed them.

When Nuclear Man got to Metropolis, he found Superman standing on the street outside Metropolis Tower, but there was no sign of Lacy.

"Where is the woman?" he demanded.

"Give it up. You'll never find her," Superman said.

"If you will not tell me, I will hurt people!" he roared. And then, he began to fulfill his promise. He sent out an energy bolt that exploded a gas pipe so it burst into flame. Another flash of energy and a car exploded. With his nuclear levitation, he lifted cars into the air.

When a police SWAT team arrived, they circled Nuclear Man and began firing at him. Their bullets bounced off him. Then he radiated so much heat that their rifle barrels melted! They were helpless against his awesome powers!

"Stop! Stop! You win!" Superman cried. "I'll take you to her."

Nuclear Man grinned triumphantly. He followed Superman to the top of the building. Nuclear Man found Superman standing guard in front of an elevator. "Where is she?" he said.

"Far away from here and safe," Superman said, but he glanced over his shoulder, as if to make sure the doors were securely closed.

It was the signal Nuclear Man had been waiting

for. He was sure Lacy was in the elevator. He lunged past Superman, forcing the elevator doors to open.

"No! Don't go in there! She's not in there!" Superman cried.

Nuclear Man ignored him. He pulled the doors open and found — *nothing*. Nothing but total darkness.

Superman's trick had worked. He slammed the elevators doors closed behind Nuclear Man, locking the villain in total darkness. He had figured out that if Nuclear Man got his power from the sun, he would be powerless in the dark. Now he had him trapped for good.

He thought.

22

As soon as the elevator door was locked, Superman took the entire mechanism and pulled it up out of the top of the building. He wanted to take the sleeping Nuclear Man to a place where nobody would ever find him and to a place where he could do no harm.

He carried the locked elevator off into space to the moon. Inside, Nuclear Man was powerless. Except for one thing. Somehow, the elevator wall had developed a small crack in it. When Superman rested the elevator on the surface of the moon, the sun's rays peeped right through the crack and onto Nuclear Man. It wasn't much, but it was enough. He soaked up the solar energy until he had enough strength to break out.

Superman was completely unaware that Nuclear Man was regaining his power. He was ready to head for home. He paused for a minute to straighten out the flag which America's last lunar astronauts had planted there. Then he saluted the flag.

At that instant, Nuclear Man attacked. He threw

Superman to the ground. Superman counterattacked, knocking Nuclear Man down. Nuclear Man recovered, and the two of them began trading mighty blows.

Finally, Nuclear Man collapsed. A very tired Superman turned to straighten out the flag again, confident he'd won this time. But he hadn't. Once again, Nuclear Man took Superman by surprise. He grabbed him in a giant bear hug. Superman couldn't fight back. Nuclear Man now completely drained Superman's energy it seemed. He then buried the unconscious Superman under moon rocks and prepared to return to Earth.

"Lacy? Laaacccyyyyyyy!" he cried as he took off.

Superman struggled to pull himself out of the dirt. Was it possible that this time he was beaten? Certainly Nuclear Man had incredible strength and amazing powers. Superman couldn't win a battle of brawn with him. But *could* he win a battle of brains?

Suddenly, Superman knew the answer. Quickly, he figured it out. He leaped into the moon's sky and then with every ounce of his super-strength, he began to move the moon! He moved it until it was exactly between the sun and Earth, blocking all sunlight from Earth. Since Nuclear Man needed sunlight for energy, the only thing Superman could do was to block the sun! The Earth was completely dark now.

Just one more thing: Superman had to find Nuclear Man and see to it that he'd never see daylight again.

Superman flew toward Earth. He found Nuclear Man hanging in the air helplessly, clutching Lacy. She was very scared. Superman released her from Nuclear Man's grip and returned her to safety.

Then Superman went to get Nuclear Man. He took the sleeping giant and brought him back to Metropolis. Near the city was a nuclear power plant. Nuclear Man might do some good *there*. Superman dropped Nuclear Man into the plant's cooling tower and slammed the hatch shut over him.

"Bull's-eye!" Superman shouted victoriously as all the lights in the city glowed brightly, fueled by Nuclear Man's power.

Then Superman returned to space to move the moon back to its own orbit. The work was done. The eclipse could end now.

23

Superman had a few loose ends to tie up. The first thing that needed to be tied up was Lex Luthor.

Lex and Lenny were trying to escape. But they couldn't escape from Superman. He found them driving down a highway at top speed. Suddenly the car flew into the air. Superman was flying them.

His first stop was at a chain gang in Florida. Superman brought Lex back where he'd come from.

"Hey, Mozart's back!" one of his fellow prisoners greeted him. Lex just grunted.

Superman's next stop was a special home for Lenny. He took Lenny to the priest in charge of the home. "This boy has been under a bad influence. Can you help him?" Superman asked.

"Every boy can be helped, Superman," the priest told him.

"That's what I think, too," Superman agreed. He left Lenny in the good man's care.

Back in Metropolis, things were looking up, too. Lois and Jimmy Olsen were watching Perry White.

He was watching workmen remove the sign which read "Warfield Publications" on the *Daily Planet* building.

"Mr. White, are you sure you know what you're doing?" Lois asked. Mr. White just smiled.

Then David Warfield arrived in his limousine. When he saw what was going on, he stormed out of the car. "You'd better have a good explanation, White!" he yelled.

Mr. White said, "You know, I'm not a tycoon. I'm just an old reporter. But I figured that whatever it was *you* did with a bunch of bankers to buy this newspaper, I could *undo* with a bunch of bankers. A lot of the bankers in town agreed with me. Now, Warfield, you're just a minority stockholder. The paper belongs to *us* now."

Lois and Jimmy could barely believe their ears. That was the best news of all to them, but they didn't have time to celebrate right then. Superman was having another press conference at the United Nations. They had to hurry to get there on time.

Lacy and Clark were sharing a taxi cab. Clark was going to the press conference. Lacy was going to the airport.

"Daddy's offered me jobs at some of his other companies, but I think I'll take some time off. I don't really think the same way Daddy does anymore, Clark. All he cares about is making money. I've learned a lot from you. I know that people have to be responsible, or others can be hurt."

Clark smiled when she said that. He could tell that she *had* changed. She had learned a lot.

"I'm going to find a place like Smallville in the country — maybe a farm. I'd like to see how good life can be," she told him.

That gave Clark an idea. "You know, Lacy, if you get to Smallville, I know a real estate agent, Leon Hornsby. He might have the perfect place for you. Tell him I sent you."

Clark knew that if the *new* Lacy Warfield bought the old Kent farm, it would be in good hands. It would never be a shopping mall.

She rolled up the window of the cab. She waved a final good-bye to Clark as the cab pulled away.

Clark pushed through the crowd by the United Nations until he found Lois and Jimmy.

"It must have been an effort to get out of bed, Clark," Lois teased him. She hadn't seen him since she'd been at his apartment.

"Well, I'm feeling a lot better," he said. "All because I had a visit from a very good nurse." Lois would never know how close to the truth that was!

Lois got down to business. "Okay, your job is to tape interviews with the crowd. I'm covering Superman's press conference."

"Oh, no!" Clark cried. "I left my new tape recorder in the taxi!" He ran back out of the crowd.

"Same old Mr. Kent," Jimmy said, laughing. "He'll never change."

"I hope not," Lois said, heading for the press conference.

24

In a gentle rush of wind, Superman arrived at the United Nations. This time, though, instead of speaking to the delegates *inside*, he was speaking to all the people of the world *outside*.

He stepped up to the microphones, which would reach every corner of Earth.

"Once more, we have survived the threat of war," Superman said. "And once more, we've found a fragile peace. I thought I could give you all the gift of peace, but it is not mine to give."

Superman looked over the crowd in front of him. Everybody was listening carefully. He continued speaking. "There will only be peace on Earth when the people want it so badly their governments will *have* to give it to them." The crowd cheered. Superman felt that the people of Earth were closer to peace than he'd ever seen them. "I wish you could all see this planet, Earth, as I see it — "

Suddenly, Superman had an idea. "Wait a minute! Maybe you *can*! I'll be right back."

Much to the surprise of everybody around the planet, Superman shot into the air in the middle

of his own press conference. Seconds later, he landed again — this time in the playground by Jeremy's school.

Jeremy and his classmates gaped at their visitor. They had just been listening to him on the radio. "I need your help, Jeremy," Superman said, taking the boy's hand.

Before he could even answer, Superman lifted him high into the air, and flew him above Earth.

Jeremy could see everything in the world as it had never been seen by a human before. It was more beautiful than he could have imagined.

"Awesome!" Jeremy gasped.

Superman held him firmly. "Jeremy, I need you to tell the people of the world what you see," he said.

"I'll try," Jeremy told him. Looking down at Earth, he began to describe the sights. "Well, I see the ocean currents, and the rain, and the mountains, and the rivers, but — " Jeremy stopped speaking for a moment.

"Go on," Superman encouraged him.

"But you can't tell where one country begins and another ends. You can't see any borders. It's just — one world."

Superman sighed happily. It was just what he'd hoped Jeremy would see. "Good," he said. "If you can see it, and I can see it, maybe some day everyone will see it!"